CW00847675

Welcome to the Disney Learning Programme!

Sharing a book with your child is the perfect opportunity to cuddle and enjoy the reading experience together. Research has shown that reading aloud with your child is one of the most important ways to prepare them for success as a reader. When you share books with each other, you help strengthen your child's reading and vocabulary skills as well as stimulate their curiosity, imagination and enthusiasm for reading.

In this book, join eight Disney Princesses as they each prepare for their royal birthdays, with plenty of lovely surprises along the way. You can enhance the reading experience by talking to your child about their own experience of birthdays and birthday surprises. What is their favourite birthday memory? What made the day so special? Children find it easier to understand what they read when they can connect it with their own personal experiences

Children learn in different ways and at different speeds, but they all require a supportive environment to nurture a lifelong love of books, reading and learning. The *Adventures in Reading* books are carefully levelled to present new challenges to developing readers. They are filled with familiar and fun characters from the wonderful world of Disney to make the learning experience comfortable, positive and enjoyable.

Enjoy your reading adventure together!

For Ruby, Lucas and Theo
– J.L.W.

© 2015 Disney Enterprises, Inc. All rights reserved.

The movie THE PRINCESS AND THE FROG Copyright © 2009 Disney,
story inspired in part by the book THE FROG PRINCESS by E.D. Baker Copyright © 2002,
published by Bloomsbury Publishing, Inc.

Scholastic Children's Books
Euston House,
24 Eversholt Street,
London NW1 1DB, UK

A division of Scholastic Ltd
London • New York • Toronto • Sydney • Auckland
Mexico City • New Delhi • Hong Kong

This book was first published in the United States by Random House Children's Books in 2012.
Published in Australia in 2014 by Scholastic Australia.
This edition published in the UK by Scholastic Ltd in 2015.

ISBN 978 1 4071 6302 4

Printed in Malaysia

2 4 6 8 10 9 7 5 3 1

Papers used by Scholastic Children's Books are made from woods grown in sustainable forests.

www.scholastic.co.uk

Royal Birthdays

ADVENTURES IN READING

By Jennifer Liberts Weinberg

Illustrated by Elisa Marrucchi

It is Belle's birthday. The Beast is throwing her a big party. There are streamers and balloons. All her friends at the castle are there.

Chip and Cogsworth blow party whistles.
Cogsworth wears a party hat. There are
lots of presents to open.

Belle's friends have made a cake. It has three layers! It is pretty and pink.

Belle cuts the cake. Everybody sings 'Happy Birthday'. Belle shares the cake with everyone.

It is Aurora's birthday. The Three
Good Fairies work hard all day.
Fauna bakes a cake.

Flora and Merryweather make a dress.
It is white and pink. It has ribbons and
a wide collar. It has long sleeves.

The birthday girl is here!
Aurora is happy to see her friends.
It is time to have a birthday party!

It is Tiana's birthday. Prince Naveen has planned a party. They go out into the garden.

Lanterns are hanging outside. They are gold and glowing. The band is playing. There are so many presents to open!

It is Cinderella's birthday. Her friends have brought her presents. They are in big and little boxes. They are tied with big ribbon bows.

Cinderella is excited. The presents look so pretty! What could be inside?

Inside the little box is a new ring.
Inside the big box is a silver crown.
Look how they sparkle!

Cinderella loves her presents.
She puts on the sparkly ring.
She puts on the sparkly crown.

It is Rapunzel's birthday.
Flynn has a present for her.
It is in a big, purple box.

Flynn has another present for Rapunzel.
It is not in a box. It is outside the castle.
Rapunzel runs to see.

Wow! Look at the lanterns!
Everyone in the kingdom has one.
They send them all into the sky.

The lanterns shine. They shine like
the stars. Rapunzel loves her present.
It is the best night ever!

It is Snow White's birthday. The Seven Dwarfs throw a party. There are big balloons. There is a big cake.

Look at all the candles! There are fourteen of them. Snow White blows them all out. Cake for everyone!

Everyone has a present for Snow White.
Some are in boxes with bows.
Sneezy has brought some flowers.

Dopey has more big balloons.
They float up in the air.
Dopey floats up with them!

It is Jasmine's birthday. Aladdin has given her lots of sweets. They fly over the town. They see all the happy children.

Jasmine shares her sweets with everyone. The children are excited! There is a party in the streets!

It is Ariel's birthday. All her friends
come to her party. They have fun.
They play party games.

They play 'Pin the Tail on the Dolphin'.
Everyone has a turn. Flounder is
going to win.

Everyone gets a party bag.
They are filled with sweets.
Now it's time for cake!

There are cupcakes for everyone.
They have rainbow sprinkles!
They are very yummy.

Happy birthday,
princesses!